Sing of the Earth and Sky

Poems about Our Planet
and the Wonders Beyond

by Aileen Fisher

Illustrated by Karmen Thompson

Wordsong
Boyds Mills

Published by Wordsong
Boyds Mills Press, Inc.
A Highlights Company
815 Church Street
Honesdale, Pennsylvania 18431
Printed in Hong Kong

U.S. Cataloging-in-Publication Data
(Library of Congress Standards)

Fisher, Aileen.
Sing of the earth and sky : poems about our planet and the wonders
beyond / by Aileen Fisher ; illustrated by Karmen Thompson. —1st ed.
[48]p. : col. ill. ; cm.
Summary: Poems about the earth, moon, sun, and stars.
ISBN 1-56397-802-4
1. Outer space — Poetry. 2. American poetry — Collections.
I. Thompson, Karmen, ill. II. Title.
811/.54 21 2001 CIP AC
99-63741

First edition, 2001
The text of this book is set in 15-point Times.

10 9 8 7 6 5 4 3 2 1

To Jennifer and Elizabeth,
who wonder.

—A. F.

Dedicated to my loyal and supportive siblings:
Laurie Jarvela and Karen Springer.

—K. T.

CONTENTS

EARTH

MOON

SUN

STARS

Earth

THE WORLD AROUND US

Sing of the Earth and sky,
sing of our lovely planet,
sing of the low and high,
of fossils locked in granite.

Sing of the strange, the known,
the secrets that surround us,
sing of the wonders shown,
and wonders still around us.

HARD TO BELIEVE

When you walk on a desert
with sand all around
or climb up a mountain
a mile above ground
or sail on an ocean
where beaches abound,
it's hard to believe
that our planet is *round*.

OUR PLANET EARTH

Don't you think that someone had
a very funny notion
to go and name our planet *Earth*
when most of it is ocean?

EARTH MEETS SKY

The fields go up
and the sky comes down
to meet in a line
at the end of town.

It's good they meet,
the blue and green,
else what would there *be*
in the space between?

OUT THERE ON EARTH

Do people (if any)
on faraway stars
or planets like Jupiter,
Pluto, or Mars
keep asking each other
(with twinkles of mirth):
"Could anyone *possibly*
live on the Earth?"

THE SPINNING EARTH

The earth, they say,
spins round and round.
It doesn't look it
from the ground,
and never makes
a spinning sound.

And water never
swirls and swishes
from oceans full
of dizzy fishes,
and shelves don't lose
their pans and dishes.

And houses don't go whirling by
or puppies swirl around the sky
or robins spin instead of fly.

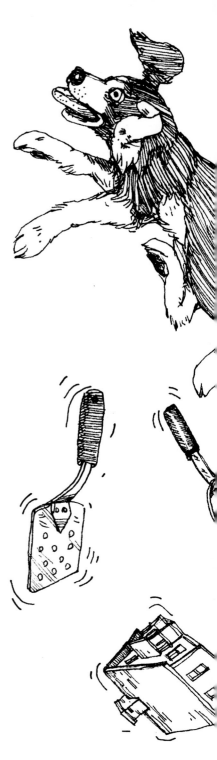

It may be true
what people say
about our spinning
night and day . . .
but I keep wondering
anyway.

13

LOOKING THROUGH SPACE

If people are living
on Venus and Mars
and looking through space
at the planets and stars,
I wonder if Earth
seems a queer sort of thing,
with whiteness in winter
and greenness in spring.

MOON

LOOKING DOWN

I wonder if
the Man in the Moon
so high above the town
sees our Earth
  as full,
  or half,
  or crescent,
looking down?

MOONS

The new moon is timid,
the new moon is shy,
it ventures just a little way
into the western sky,
then eases back behind the hill
and shuts its squinty eye.

The full moon is fearless,
the full moon is spry—
it clambers up and saunters down
the mountains of the sky
and doesn't stop all night to rest
or shut its shiny eye.

TWO MOONS

When astronauts describe the moon
they make it sound quite dreary.
"It's cold and dead and desolate,"
they tell you if you query.

But that sounds very strange to me . . .
how *can* it be so dreary?
Whenever I look up at it,
the moon is bright and cheery.

AT DUSK

The sun goes down,
and none too soon.
Here come the stars!
Here comes the moon!

MOONSTRUCK

I'd like to see rabbits
under the moon,
dancing in winter,
dancing in June,
dancing around
while twilight lingers
and blinky-eyed stars
look down through their fingers.

I'd like to see rabbits
under the moon,
but I always,
always
have to go to bed too soon.

EARLY MOON

Some days the moon comes early,
at least an hour or two.
Her watch is wrong, or maybe
she hasn't much to do.

I've seen her palely waiting
upon a sky-blue shelf,
so white and sort of lonely
she isn't like herself.

But when the sun sinks westward,
and evening comes, and night,
she reaches out an eager hand
and switches on her light.

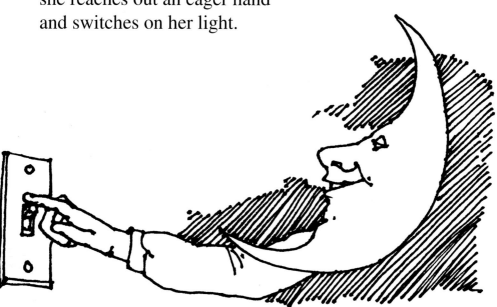

OLD MAN MOON

The moon is very, very old.
The reason why is clear:
he gets a birthday once a month
instead of once a year.

COMMA IN THE SKY

A comma hung above the park,
a shiny punctuation mark;
we saw it curving in the dark
the night the moon was new.

A period hung above the bay,
immense though it was far away;
we saw it at the end of day
the night the moon was full.

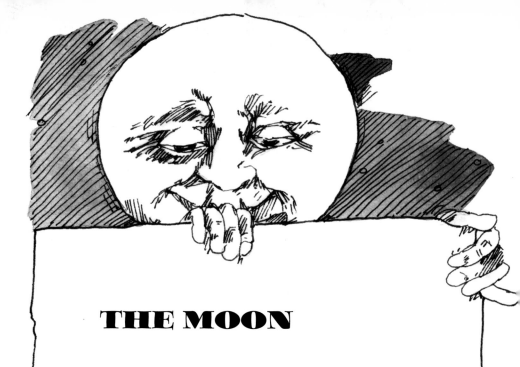

THE MOON

My puppy looks at the big old moon
after the day turns dim
and probably thinks it's a bright balloon
with a face inside the rim.
He doesn't know about astronauts . . .
the moon hasn't changed for *him.*

DAY AND NIGHT

When the sky begins changing
her dress for the night,
she does it so slowly
you can't see it quite.

But when she removes
from her velvety pocket
the silvery moon
that she wears for a locket,

And bright little sequins
of stars sparkle out,
you know Day is over
and Night is about.

SUN

SUNBURST

When Sun
spills out its gold,
too much
for it to hold,
it gilds
the hills and valleys
and even
paves the alleys . . .
and makes
our coats and collars
look like
a million dollars.

27

LONELY

The sun, I think, is lonely
because it's one-and-only—
there's not a single other sun
in sight.

The moon is never lonely.
It, too, is one-and-only,
but it has stars to neighbor with
at night.

28

THE EYE OF THE SKY

The face of the sky
has a golden eye
by day, when the sun
is low or high.

The face of the sky
has a silver eye
at night, when the moon
goes sailing by.

All day, all night,
with a watch to keep,
how does the sky
have a chance to *sleep*?

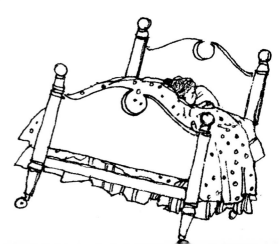

SUN PRINTS

The lawn is full of footprints,
golden tracks that show
where the sun went walking
a day or two ago.

My father calls them *dandelions*.
I think they're sun prints, though.

MIRRORS

The sun must have a lot of fun
from dawn of day till day is done,

Seeing its bright and shiny face
in every puddle every place.

31

HOW BIG?

The sun, they say, is very big,
a star that shines by day,
much bigger than the whole big earth,
oh, *very* much, they say.

But when I'm hiding in a field
of clover-smelling hay,
a single little clover plant
can hide the sun away.

THE SUN

Every day coming,
every day going,
bringing a goldness
out of the black,

Every day climbing
over the heavens,
sinking at sunset,
soon to be back,

Coming and going,
going and coming,
leaving no footprint,
leaving no track.

IN THE SUN AND SHADOW

The hands of the sun
are warm on me
when I walk in the open meadow,

But the hands feel cool
when I pass a tree
and walk through the leafy shadow.

34

THE QUIET-SHINING SUN

After the gusty, dusty wind
that blustered out of space
has whipped the grass
and flipped the boughs
and made the meadow race,

I see the quiet sun come out
and, with a patient face,
serenely pick the scenery up
and put it back in place.

STARS

THE COUNTLESS STARS

Suppose you stood
on a darkened slope
and looked at the sky
through a telescope
and counted the stars
for hours . . . or, say,
you counted a night
of your life away . . .

You'd just make a *start,*
a very small try,
at counting the number
of stars in the sky.

THE NEAREST STAR

Which is the star
of middle-size
that's nearest to the Earth?

We don't know much
about its age
or much about its birth.

We know it's not
like other stars
that show when day is done:

It shines BY DAY
from far away
and has a name . . . THE SUN.

STAR PRINTS

In winter when the moon is high
and has a dazzling glow
I think the stars must leave the sky
to play upon the snow;
for in the morning every lawn
has such a twinkly glare
it seems a million shiny stars
have left their footprints there.

WOULDN'T YOU THINK?

With so many stars
out there in space,
too many to count,
too many to trace,
wouldn't you think
a few might show
green grass growing
or tracks in snow?

I wonder if people
will ever know.

40

LITTLE STARS

Wouldn't you think
little stars might
get very tired
staying up all night?

UNTIL WE BUILT A CABIN

When we lived in a city
(three flights up and down)
I never dreamed how many stars
could show above a town.

When we moved to a village
where lighted streets were few,
I thought I could see ALL the stars,
but, oh, I never knew . . .

Until we built a cabin
where hills are high and far,
I never knew how many
                many
                    stars there really are.

43

SHOOTING STARS

When stars get loosened
in their sockets,
they shoot off through
the night like rockets.
But though I stay
and watch their trip
and search where they
have seemed to slip,
I never yet have found a CHIP
for any of my pockets.

44

STARS

It's very hard,
oh, very hard
to cut a paper star,

And so I blink
each time I think
how many stars there are.

I look up high
and think, "Oh, my,
the stars are bright and fine,

But who had time
to make them all
and get them all to shine?"

UP THERE IN THE DARK

Stars come out
at eight or nine
(in fall at six or seven),

Stars, of course,
come out to shine
to light the way to heaven,

For, otherwise,
it wouldn't show
up there in the dark, you know.

46

A SHOOTING STAR

Wish upon a shooting star.
I watch.
I wait.
How few there are!

And then at last
a bright one flashes
down the sky
and turns to ashes
before I even
blink my lashes.

Wish upon a shooting star.
It comes so fast
from off so far
I can't think what
my wishes *are*
for wishing on
a shooting star.

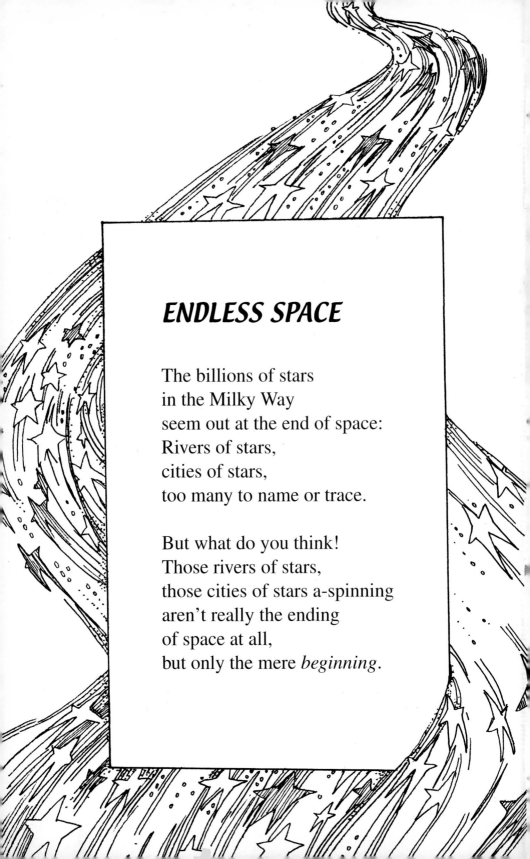

ENDLESS SPACE

The billions of stars
in the Milky Way
seem out at the end of space:
Rivers of stars,
cities of stars,
too many to name or trace.

But what do you think!
Those rivers of stars,
those cities of stars a-spinning
aren't really the ending
of space at all,
but only the mere *beginning*.